Maggie &
Davis Mann

The world is a better place
when we share. Be kind
always!

♡ Melody

ISBN: 978-1-7377151-5-3

Library of Congress Control Number: 2021921501

Illustration by Yulia Tomenko
Edited by Victoria Augustine

First Printing edition 2022

www.ada-ari.com

For Kosi

You brought new meaning to my life

Mbekwu the turtle is cunning and slow.
He carries his home wherever he goes.

His home is a shell.

You see it has cracks.

Well, here is the story that goes way way back.

The birds had a party high up in the sky,
But turtles could not go for they could not fly.
"I have an idea!" the owl then said
"Let's lend feathers to Mbekwu our friend."
The birds loved that idea and before you knew,
Mbekwu had wings and away they flew.

The party was filled with fun and good food,
And cunning Mbekwu was up to no good.
He said to his friends, "Let's play a new game.
"While here at the party, let's each pick
nicknames."

"Call me Singer" the nightingale said.
"Tree-top!" said woodpecker to all his friends.
The birds picked nicknames, and thought "This is fun!"

Mbekwu smiled and said "Call me EVERYONE."

His bird friends thought "Hmm. What a strange name.
But what does it matter? Let's play some more games!"

And boy did they play! On slides and swings
See saws, trampolines, and other fun things.

At lunch time, the bird king sounded the gong.
They ran to the food spread, yummy and long
But just then, Mbekwu called out to the king"
"Who is the food for?" he said with a wink.

"It's for EVERYONE" the bird king declared.
And all of a sudden, the birds looked quite scared.
"My name's EVERYONE! This food is for me!"
Said Mbekwu. Greedy and cunning was he.

The birds looked on as Mbekwu ate
And ate and ate, and cleared the plates.
A little bit sad, the birds then decided
To head for the drinks that the king provided.

Mbekwu looked up, appearing quite proud. He said to the king in a voice rather loud. "Who are these drinks for, oh royal king?" His question had quite a familiar ring

"They're for EVERYONE!" the king replied

Mbekwu walked over, beaming with pride.
The birds just watched, hungry, thirsty and sad.
Then decided to leave before getting mad.

Mbekwu did not mind, his stomach was fed.
"I'll play by myself!" He selfishly said.
Mbekwu did not see that, as the birds left,
They each took their feathers that kept his shell dressed.

"If I flap my arms, perhaps I can fly."
Mbekwu then thought, as he leaped to the sky.
But try as he might with all of that flapping,
Mbekwu could not fly, he was quickly....

CRACK !!!

"Oh no!" he wailed, his shell was in pieces
The birds heard the sound and came for a visit
"I am so sorry," Mbekwu cried "I should have shared.
From now on, I'll be a good friend." He declared.

The birds glued his shell back, piece by piece.
It all came together with some elbow grease.